5 Minute
KITTEN
TALES

Meet the Little Kittens!

When a mother cat has *five* little kittens to take care of,
she certainly has her paws full!

Honeybun

Rolypoly

Tiger Tail

Fluffy

Mopsy

5 MINUTE KITTEN TALES

WRITTEN BY NICOLA BAXTER
ILLUSTRATED BY JENNY PRESS

ARMADILLO

This edition published in 2002
by Armadillo Books
an imprint of
Bookmart Limited
Registered Number 2372865
Desford Road
Enderby
Leicester
LE9 5AD

ISBN 1-84322-114-4

Printed in Slovakia

Contents

Where's That Kitten?

When a mother cat has *five* little kittens to take care of, she certainly has her paws full! She just can't keep her eyes on all of them at once.

One morning, Mamma Cat was busy giving her babies their breakfast. "One bowl of porridge for you, and one for you, and one for you, and one for you, and one... Just a minute, where's that kitten?" The fifth little kitten was nowhere to be seen.

Mamma Cat looked under the beds and in the closets. She checked in the laundry basket and hunted through the toy box. But there was no little kitten to be found.

"Now then," said Mamma Cat, "one of you kittens must know where your brother is. Well, Fluffy?"

"I don't know," mewed Fluffy.

"What about you, Rolypoly?"

"I haven't seen him at all."

"And have you seen your brother, Mopsy," asked her mother, "with your bright little eyes?"

"No, Mamma," said Mopsy.

But when Mamma Cat turned to Honeybun, it was as plain as could be that the kitten knew *something*.

6

"Well?" asked Mamma Cat.

"He's gone on an adventure," explained Honeybun.

"An adventure? What sort of an adventure?"

"He's ... well ... it's a *climbing* adventure...."

Mamma Cat frowned and sighed. "A climbing adventure indeed! I hope he took an oxygen mask."

"W-what?" stammered Honeybun.

"In very high places, the air is really thin," explained Mamma Cat. "It would be difficult for a little kitten to breathe without extra oxygen. And that could be very, very dangerous."

Before Honeybun could say another word, they all heard a plaintive little sound.

"Help!" called someone from a very high place. "Help! Meow! Help!"

Mamma Cat didn't need to look around. She reached straight up to the top of the closet and scooped up one frightened little kitten.

"Well, Tiger Tail," she said, "your climbing is certainly very good. But didn't you *want* any breakfast?"

"Oh," said poor Tiger Tail, "my climbing *up* is very good, but my climbing *down* needs more practice. And, of course, without oxygen…"

"I have heard," said Mamma Cat with a smile, "that porridge is just as good as oxygen in some situations. No more climbing, please, until *after* breakfast!"

7

Tiger Tail Trouble

Some little kittens, like some little children, just can't help getting into trouble. They try as hard as they can to be good. They don't mean to throw pudding over visiting cats—but still Great Aunt Flora has to wash her whiskers. They do take care of their clothes—but still one glove, one sock, and a woolly hat with a pompom on top get stuck at the top of a tree. They run as fast as they can to get home in time for supper, but still Mamma Cat is waiting grimly on the doorstep with a plate of burnt sausages.

Tiger Tail was a kitten just like that. His father had taken him aside for a Serious Talk more than once, but still Tiger Tail got into trouble almost every day.

One morning, Tiger Tail looked at the calendar and saw that it was Mother's Day. Fluffy, Rolypoly, Mopsy, and Honeybun all had little presents for Mamma Cat, and they had put their pawprints on a pretty card.

"What kind kittens you all are," said Mamma Cat, as her little ones crowded around her.

Tiger Tail hid behind the chair. He had *meant* to remember. Quietly, he slipped out to buy a present.

Oh dear! Even when he was trying to do something good, Tiger Tail got into trouble. First he got caught on a thornbush and tore his trousers. Then, as he was looking over his shoulder to see whether his underpants were showing, he fell into a muddy puddle. And as he tried to clean himself up, the penny he had been clutching rolled out of his paw and fell into a little stream by the road.

It was late and beginning to get dark as Tiger Tail arrived home. Mamma Cat was waiting anxiously at the door as one tired and muddy little kitten threw himself into her arms and sobbed out the whole sorry story.

But Mamma Cat gave him a big kiss and squeezed him tight. "The best present of all is knowing that you are safe and sound, Tiger Tail," she said with a smile. "But what *have* you done to your trousers?"

The Great Escape

L ots of kittens like to collect something. It may be stamps, or shells, or leaves. At school, all the little kittens loved to show each other their latest finds.

"This is a very rare giant oyster shell," said Mopsy. "It might even have a pearl in it!"

"This is an even rarer triangle-shaped blue stamp from Gala-gala-land," said her friend Amybell.

"I've got a new dinosaur picture for my collection," said Honeybun. "It's a catosaurus!"

Even Tiger Tail, who preferred climbing trees to collecting things, had a very interesting box of feathers he'd found on his many fur-raising adventures.

Only George did not have a collection. It seemed that everything he was interested in was already collected by someone else. Then, one morning, as he was digging in the garden for his Granny, he had an idea. "There is one thing I am *really* interested in," he said to himself. "I'll start collecting today."

But George decided he would not tell anyone about his collection until it was really impressive. He kept it in his locker at school to keep it safe.

Unfortunately, George did not know that the lockers were cleaned every week. And the cleaner left his door ever so slightly open....

Next morning, Mrs. Mumbles, the teacher, was busy showing the class some special number work when she suddenly gave a great shriek.

"Oooooh!" she cried. "Oooooooooh! Something slimy and slithery has squiggled down my neck!"

At the same moment, Mopsy jumped onto her desk. "Something wet and wiggly is sitting on my book!"

In no time at all, everyone was shouting at once. "The pencils are coming to life!" cried Honeybun, who always had a rather vivid imagination.

Only George was calm. "Stop!" he shouted. "You'll frighten them!"

At that moment, all the kittens and Mrs. Mumbles stopped shouting and turned to look at George.

"It's just my collection," he explained. "They won't hurt you."

"I know I'm going to be sorry I asked you this, George," said Mrs. Mumbles, "but what *exactly* did you collect?"

"Worms!" smiled George. "I had seventeen of them!"

It took *ages* for the class to find all the wriggly, wiggly worms. Can you find them any quicker?

Bella's Birthday

Most kittens are friendly and fun, but once in a while you may meet a kitten who is just a little too big for her boots. When Bella invited all the other kittens to her birthday party, she made sure they knew it would be the biggest and best party ever.

"I'm having a huge cake," she crowed. "And there will be giant balloons and a magician."

"It's a pity he can't make *her* disappear," whispered Rolypoly to Fluffy, "just for a while, anyway."

Bella lived in a very grand house, with columns either side of the door. When the kittens arrived, she greeted them in a dress that was so covered with ribbons and bows she could hardly move.

"Do come in," she said. "But please wipe your paws carefully. You poorer kittens may not be used to fine carpets."

Tiger Tail and Honeybun almost turned back right then, but they were curious about the magician and even more curious about the huge cake, so they joined their friends in the party room.

It would have been a lovely party, if Bella had not tried to show off at every opportunity. Even the magician, Mr. Kat, got tired of her comments.

"I know how *that's* done," she said loudly, as he produced a bunch of flowers from a hat.

Mr. Kat was tempted to ask Bella to take over, if she was so smart, but after all, it *was* her birthday.

"Now, listen to me!" called Bella, as everyone applauded at the end of the show. "Come into the garden, please, to watch me being photographed."

The kittens trooped outside, where Melinda Felini, the famous photographer, was waiting.

"Perhaps you'd like to hold these giant balloons, Bella," she suggested.

Bella grasped the bunch of balloons and smiled her widest smile … just as a gust of wind blew around the corner of the house.Up, up, and away went the birthday kitten!

Some say that Mr. Kat used magic to make that wind blow. Some say that Melinda Felini had photographed Bella before and had not enjoyed it. Some say that Bella was a kind and quiet kitten ever after. But I believe I can hear her voice even now….

"Oh, haven't you tried ballooning, Mrs. Mumbles? It's the *only* way to travel!"

The Package Problem

One autumn day, Mamma Cat really didn't feel too well. She sneezed and she sniffled as she sat in her chair.

"Don't worry, little ones," she said to her kittens. "It's only a cold, but I really don't think I should go outside today."

"No, no," said Mopsy. "You stay inside where it's warm and we'll do everything."

Mamma Cat looked a little doubtful. Last time the kittens had tried to help, she had spent three weeks putting things back in order. In fact, her knitting had been all tangled up ever since Honeybun had "finished" the sleeve of a sweater. But the little kittens looked so eager to help, and she did feel awful, so she agreed.

"I'll tell Fluffy and Rolypoly how to make dinner," she said. "Mopsy can make the beds, and Tiger Tail and Honeybun can take this package to Farmer Feather. It's his birthday."

Tiger Tail and Honeybun carried the package between them. It wasn't heavy, but it was an awkward shape. It was too far across for one little kitten to stretch his arms around it.

As soon as they got outside, the two kittens realized they had a big problem. The wind seemed to love that package! First it blew on it so hard that Tiger Tail and Honeybun could hardly hold on. Then they were pushed across the lane and into the hedge. As they came around the corner near Farmer Feather's farm, they found that the wind had somehow sneaked around behind them, and was blowing them past the farmhouse!

As they staggered into the barnyard, the wind played one last trick. It caught hold of the string on the package and wrapped it around the gatepost, so that it took Tiger Tail ten minutes to untangle it. (Honeybun never had been any good at untangling things, as Mamma Cat's knitting still showed!)

Farmer Feather was delighted with his present. It was too large to go through the doorway, so he opened it in the yard.

"Be careful," warned Honeybun. "The wind seems to want to play with it. It might fly away!"

But Farmer Feather laughed. "Oh no," he said. "The wind can play with it every day and it will never fly away. It's the most beautiful weather vane I've ever seen!"

Curious Kittens

Tiger Tail kicked at a leaf lying on the path. "I'm bored," he said. "We've played all our usual games."

The kittens were all outside on a beautiful sunny day, while Mamma Cat had some friends visiting.

"You kittens can stay outside," she had said, "so that we can have a little peace."

"Let's go down to Farmer Feather's farm," suggested Honeybun. "We can see what his weather vane looks like on the farmhouse."

So Mopsy poked her head through the doorway to tell Mamma Cat where they were going, and the five little kittens set off for the farm.

They came across Farmer Feather working on his tractor in a field before they reached the farmhouse. "Yes, you can go and look," he said, "but whatever you do, don't open the barn door."

Down at the farmhouse, the kittens thought the weather vane looked lovely.

"Now what?" asked Rolypoly. Tiger Tail didn't answer. He was looking at the barn.

The other kittens looked too.

"I wonder what is in there," said Rolypoly.

"So do I," said Fluffy.

"But we mustn't …" whispered Mopsy, "or at least, only very, very quickly."

Those five naughty kittens crept up to the barn door. They tried to peek in through the slats of wood, but they couldn't see anything.

"All right," said Rolypoly. "Let's open the door just a tiny, tiny bit."

Fluffy stood on tiptoes to open the latch. Then she pulled the door toward her ever so gently.

Squawk! Cluck! Quark! The kittens tumbled backward as twenty fluttering fowls rushed out of the barn.

There were hens everywhere, and just at that moment Farmer Feather came home. He was *not* happy.

"You kittens will just have to help me catch them," he said, rushing around the barnyard.

When they had finished, the kittens were out of breath but smiling. It had been great fun running after those skittering chickens. "Maybe we could let them out again sometime," giggled Honeybun.

Farmer Feather flopped down, panting. "Don't … even … *think* … about … it," he gasped.

The Pawprint Puzzle

For one whole week, the little kittens had been cooped up inside, while outside the wind blew and snow fell and the air was cold enough to freeze your whiskers.

While they were indoors, the kittens spent a lot of time pretending to be detectives. They solved the Mystery of the Missing Sock and the Puzzle of the Disappearing Pudding. Fluffy found her lost train set, and Honeybun found a lot of cobwebs in a cupboard.

At last Mamma Cat looked out and said, "The snow has stopped, and the sun is shining. Put on your mittens and go outside."

Tiger Tail was ready first. He slipped out of the back door with a smile. "Come and find me when you're ready!" he called.

When the other little kittens opened the front door, Tiger Tail was nowhere to be seen. The kittens called, but there was no answer. Where could he have gone?

"I know," said Honeybun. "We can be detectives again and follow his pawprints in the snow!" A nice clear set of prints led away from the back door. They led down the path and up to the gate. And there they stopped. All around, the snow was smooth and gleaming white.

"He must have opened the gate," said Fluffy. But the gate had not been disturbed.

"Maybe he jumped over," said Rolypoly. But there were no footprints at all on the other side of the gate—or anywhere else!

At last Mopsy made an important announcement. "If he didn't go through, or over, or along … he went up!"

Four little kittens looked up at the blue sky. There were no clouds. There were no planes. There were no balloons, or kites, or gliders. There most definitely was no Tiger Tail.

At that moment, they heard a giggling sound. It was Tiger Tail!

"Foiled again, great detectives!" he chortled. "It's simple. I walked to the gate, and then I walked back again … backward! I put my paws in the prints I'd made before. Ha! Ha!"

Splat! A snowball hit Tiger Tail on the nose, and for the next half-hour, the great detectives had lots of fun taking their revenge!

The Picnic Pie

One sunny day, Mamma Cat had a surprise for the little kittens. "We're all going into the woods for a picnic," she said. "And if you will make some sandwiches, I will make a special pie for us."

"Can it be a cherry pie, Mamma?" asked Tiger Tail. "Cherry pie is what I like best, even if it does make my whiskers pink!"

"Oh no, Mamma," chorused Fluffy and Honeybun. "We like apple pie best. There are two of us, so it should be apple."

"There are two of us, too," cried Mopsy and Rolypoly, "and we like plum pie best."

"What am I going to do with you?" sighed Mamma Cat. "We'll ask your father what he likes best, and that is what we'll have. Then there will be no arguments."

At that moment, Father Cat came in from the garden with a basket of fruit.

"Daddy," cried Mopsy, "what kind of pie do you like best? Mamma says she'll make it!"

Father Cat smiled at Mamma Cat. "What a treat," he said. "Well, I don't mind. Whatever you like, sweetheart. All your pies are delicious!"

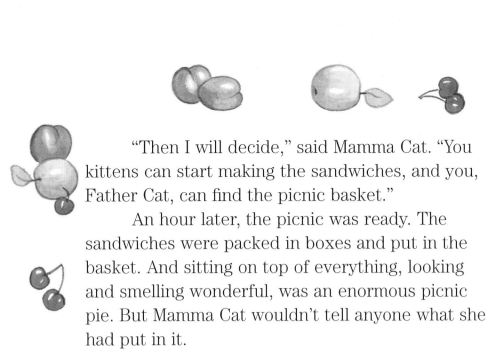

"Then I will decide," said Mamma Cat. "You kittens can start making the sandwiches, and you, Father Cat, can find the picnic basket."

An hour later, the picnic was ready. The sandwiches were packed in boxes and put in the basket. And sitting on top of everything, looking and smelling wonderful, was an enormous picnic pie. But Mamma Cat wouldn't tell anyone what she had put in it.

"You'll find out soon enough," she said.

It was lovely walking through the trees and even nicer when they sat down to munch their sandwiches. Then it was time for the famous pie. Mamma Cat cut slices for everyone and handed them out on paper plates.

"Just don't say anything until you've tasted it," she said.

Tiger Tail took a bite. "It *is* cherry!" he cried. "Thank you, Mamma."

"But there are some apples in it too," grinned Fluffy and Honeybun.

"And plums," shouted Mopsy and Rolypoly.

"It's a mixed-fruit pie," smiled Mamma. "There's something for everyone."

"You know," said Father Cat with his mouth full, "I've just remembered. *This* is the kind of pie I like best!"

It's a Monster!

There are lots of exciting things to do at school, but sometimes those naughty little kittens just didn't want to do as they were told. One day, Mrs. Mumbles, their teacher, asked them to do some reading practice, but the kittens really didn't want to sit still and read.

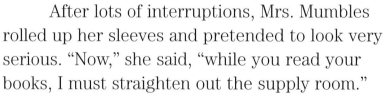

After lots of interruptions, Mrs. Mumbles rolled up her sleeves and pretended to look very serious. "Now," she said, "while you read your books, I must straighten out the supply room."

"No, no!" cried the kittens. "We can do it!" They had secretly all wanted to find out what was kept behind the supply room door.

"All right," said Mrs. Mumbles uncertainly. "But there are all kinds of things in there, so I want you little kittens to be very, very careful. Some supplies can be dangerous."

The kittens looked surprised. Dangerous? What could there be that would be dangerous?

"Maybe there are kitten-eating spiders in there," whispered Bella. "I'd better stay out here."

"There might be something old and green," suggested George, whose mother was always warning him about leaving half-eaten cakes under his bed. "It would be very smelly and…"

"Yes, yes," interrupted Honeybun quickly. "But I've thought of something even worse it might be. It might be … *a monster*!"

"They do often live in small dark places," agreed Tiger Tail. "We're going to have to be very, very careful."

So the bravest kittens—Tiger Tail, Mopsy, and George—crept into the supply room. It was very dark, and huge piles of books and equipment towered overhead. As they reached the back of the tiny room, George fell over a bucket. A mop and a swimming towel went flying, and an old drum went BOOM!

The three brave kittens had never run so fast in their lives. "It *is* a monster!" they shouted. "It's got floppy hair and flappy arms and it goes BOOM! Shut the door quick!"

Mrs. Mumbles came along to find a whole class of kittens reading very nicely from their books. She gave a small smile to herself. Well, well. So the mop-and-bucket monster trick had worked again this year!

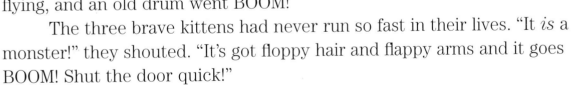
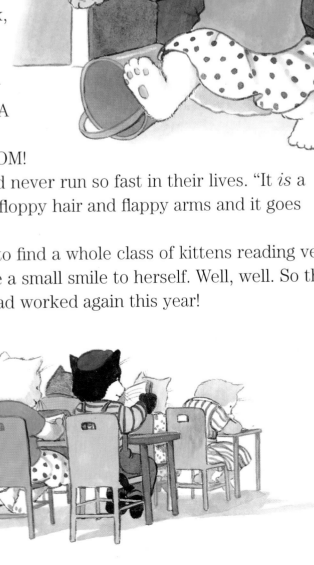

Now Remember...

Mamma Cat looked at the clock. She knew that she had to mail her letters now or it would be too late. But Father Cat wasn't home yet and Honeybun, Rolypoly, Tiger Tail, and Mopsy were playing on the floor.

"I just don't know what to do," said Mamma Cat. "It's very important that these letters are sent today."

"We'll be all right, Mamma," said Mopsy. "Daddy will be home soon, and we will be good."

"Well, I suppose you are old enough to take care of yourselves for a few minutes," Mamma Cat agreed. "But you must promise that you won't open the door for anyone, except Father, of course."

"We promise!" said the kittens. So Mamma Cat put on her coat and hurried off to the post office.

She had only been gone for a few minutes when there was a tapping at the door.

"Let me in! Let me in!" called a little voice.

It was Fluffy, who had just come home from her piano lesson. The front door could only be opened from the inside.

The kittens looked at each other. "We promised not to open the door," said Rolypoly anxiously, "except for Daddy."

"But it's starting to rain," cried Mopsy. "Poor Fluffy will get wet, and you know how long it takes to dry *her* fur!"

"But we promised…" Rolypoly was so upset he was almost crying.

Then Tiger Tail had one of his Good Ideas. "We promised not to open the door," he said, "but we didn't promise anything *at all* about the window!"

And that is why, when Mamma Cat and Father Cat arrived home at almost the same moment a little while later, they found Fluffy's little legs waving out of the window, where she was well and truly stuck!

Poor Fluffy was soon rescued, and the little kittens explained what had happened. For a moment they thought that Mamma Cat was going to be angry, but then she smiled.

"Poor little kittens," she said. "All the time I was telling you to *remember* your promise, I'd *forgotten* something very important myself. It's a good thing I stopped at the bakery on the way home to get you a treat."

Mamma Cat had bought some delicious pastries for everyone.

"And Fluffy can choose first," laughed Tiger Tail, "as long as she doesn't choose the cherry bun!"

The Treehouse

Most little kittens love to climb trees. They can't resist finding out what they can see from the highest branches, even if they do wave and wiggle in the wind. But climbing down trees is a different matter. That is something that kittens prefer not to do, which is why they so often get stuck.

The little kittens loved to visit the woods and climb the highest trees, but after the fifth time he was called out to make a daring rescue, Father Cat put his paw down.

"You kittens are just going to have to find some other way to have fun in the woods," he said. "One day I may be away when you need rescuing. Now I must go back to the house. Farmer Feather is lending me his ladder so that I can fix the roof."

There was something about the word "ladder" that gave Mopsy the tingling feeling that often means a Really Good Idea is about to arrive.

"Quiet!" she called. "I need quiet! Let me think."

The kittens knew what that meant. Mopsy's brain cells were working overtime, and they must keep out of the way.

The kittens did not have to wait long. Mopsy's whiskers began to wiggle. Her ears twitched. Her bright little eyes sparkled.

"She's got an idea!" cried Rolypoly, who knew the signs.

"We," said Mopsy grandly, "are going to build a treehouse."

It was such a Really Good Idea that the other little kittens didn't hesitate. They set off at once for Farmer Feather's wood-shed to … well … *borrow* some of Farmer Feather's wood.

Considering that five little architects helped with the plans, and five little builders hoisted and hammered, and five little painters splished and sploshed, the treehouse was finished in an amazingly short time. It did look unlike any other treehouse you have ever seen, to be sure, but it was snug, and cheerful, and in a tree —what more could a kitten wish for?

The little kittens have decided to keep the treehouse a secret for now, but Father Cat is already very suspicious about the painty pawprints on his path. He wonders if they could have anything to do with the mysterious disappearance of Farmer Feather's ladder…

Oh, Pickles!

One morning, Mamma Cat received a letter. "Your cousin Pickles is coming to stay," she said, looking at her own five little kittens.

There was silence for a moment.

"Over my dead body!" cried Father Cat, leaping to his feet. "Do you remember last time? I had to replumb the bathroom, retile the kitchen, put up a new fence, and apologize to all the cats for miles around for things that kitten had done. I'm not going through all that again."

The little kittens agreed. They liked their cousin, but it was pretty risky having him to stay.

"I'm afraid we don't have much choice," said Mamma Cat. "My sister is really not well. Someone must take care of Pickles. Besides, this letter was mailed a week ago. He's already on his way."

"Then we must batten down the hatches," said Father Cat grimly, "and get ready."

The kittens took him at his word. They hid their nicest toys and put anything that was breakable well out of reach.

"That's going too far!" laughed Mamma Cat, when Father Cat came in wearing an old army helmet. "He's not that bad!"

And the funny thing was that Pickles was not bad at all. He was polite to his uncle and aunt and he sat down at the table as meekly as any kitten you have ever seen.

"Well, Pickles," said Father Cat. "You really seem to have changed. You … er … certainly made your presence felt last time you were here."

"Oh, " smiled Pickles. "I was little then. I'm much more grown up now. Thank you for a lovely dinner. I think I'll go to bed early after my trip."

Pickles stood up and turned away. Unfortunately, the tablecloth had been tucked in his belt. In one quick motion, the plates, the saucers, the casserole, and Mamma Cat's famous marmalade pudding went hurtling across the room.

"Oh, Pickles!" cried Father Cat, Mamma Cat, and the five kittens, with tears of laughter rolling down their cheeks. "You haven't changed at all!"

Ssssh!

One night, when all the kittens and their parents were fast asleep, Tiger Tail woke up with a start. He was sure that he had heard something. Maybe it was burglars! He crept bravely out of bed and went to investigate.

But as Tiger Tail went out into the hallway, the bedroom door closed with a loud *click*!

The next thing Tiger Tail knew, Fluffy was creeping along the hallway too.

"I thought I heard a noise like a *click*," she whispered.

"That was me," said Tiger Tail. "Ssssh!"

But Fluffy had already knocked an apple out of the fruit bowl. It fell with a *thud*!

Seconds later, Rolypoly tiptoed out into the hallway to meet them.

"I thought I heard a kind of *thud*," he said.

"That was me," said Fluffy. "Ssssh!"

But Rolypoly had already bumped into a bookshelf. A book fell over with a *wumph*!

Almost at once, Mopsy crept out to join the other kittens.

"I thought I heard a sort of *wumph* noise," she whispered.

"That was me," said Rolypoly. "Ssssh!"

But Rolypoly didn't notice his father's shoes standing by the door. One of them went skidding across the floor and hit the wall with a *thwack*!

Honeybun came creeping along to join them.

"I thought I heard a *thwack*!" he hissed.

"That was me," said Rolypoly. "Ssssh!"

But Honeybun had slipped on the mat. He fell over with a *thump*!

Mamma Cat came hurrying out of her room.

"I thought I heard a *thump*," she said.

"That was me," replied Honeybun. "Ssssh!"

They all listened. There was a very quiet munching sound coming from the kitchen.

"Follow me," said Mamma Cat, picking up an umbrella.

She flung open the kitchen door. There sat Father Cat, with a huge sandwich.

"Just a little midnight snack!" he cried guiltily.

"Sssssh!" said the brave burglar-beaters. "We're trying to *sleep*, you know!"

The Lost Letter

One wet morning, Honeybun could not find the hood for his raincoat. "The other kittens had better start out for school without you," said Mamma Cat. "You can catch up with them when you find your hood. It must be around here somewhere."

Five minutes later, the kitten found his missing hood.

"You won't be late if you hurry," said Mamma Cat.

As Honeybun was running down the lane, he met the mailcat, Mr. String.

"I've got a letter for your mother," said Mr. String. "Will you take it for her?"

Honeybun took the letter and carefully put it in his pocket. He would give it to Mamma Cat that afternoon after school.

But when he came home from school that day, Honeybun forgot all about the letter. As luck would have it, the weather was sunny for ages afterward. It was about six weeks later that Honeybun put on his raincoat again and felt the paper crinkling under his paw.

The kitten felt dreadful. What if it was something important? He took the letter out of his pocket and read the big red writing on the front. "YOU ARE A WINNER!" it said. "CLAIM NOW OR LOSE YOUR PRIZE!"

Honeybun felt sick. He imagined the huge amount of money that his carelessness might have lost. Or maybe it was a car! Or a trip to the sunshine! His family would never forgive him.

Honeybun panicked. Maybe no one ever had to know. He hid the letter and went to school.

But all day Honeybun felt awful. It was as if he had a heavy weight in his tummy.

As he walked home, Honeybun knew what he had to do. He took the letter straight to Mamma Cat.

"I'm sorry," he sobbed, as he explained.

Mamma Cat put her arm around her little one. "It was just a mistake, honey," she said. "Let's see what this silly thing is about."

Honeybun couldn't understand why Mamma Cat laughed and laughed when she read the letter.

"Well done, Honeybun," she said, between giggles. "We would have won a lifetime's supply of Purple Fizz, and you know how we all hate that yucky drink. You saved us from being purple fizzily flooded!"

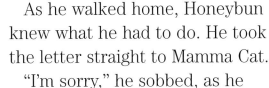

Who's Who?

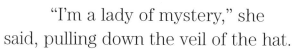

The little kittens had gone to see an exciting movie. When they got home, they could only think of one thing.

"Let's play spies!" suggested Tiger Tail.

"We'll need to disguise ourselves," said Mopsy.

So the five little kittens went off to find disguises.

One of the kittens found a sheet, a pillowcase, and an old belt.

"I'm going to disguise myself as an Arab sheik," he said, putting on some dark glasses.

Another little kitten crept into Mamma Cat's bedroom. She found a huge hat, and a coat, and some shoes.

"I'm a lady of mystery," she said, pulling down the veil of the hat.

The third little kitten went to Father Cat's chest of drawers. He found some trousers, and a jacket, and an old-fashioned hat.

I'm a double agent," he said. And he put on his dark glasses.

In Mamma Cat's sewing box, another little kitten found some beautiful silk fabric. She wound it around herself.

"I'm a princess from India," she said, pulling the silk across her nose.

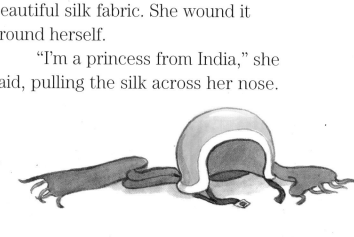

The last little kitten couldn't decide what disguise to wear. Then he saw Father Cat's coveralls on the washing machine. He put a scarf over his nose and a helmet on his head.

"I'm a racing driver," he said.

The kittens had a wonderful time playing spies that afternoon, until Mamma Cat and Father Cat came home from shopping.

"Who's been in my room, borrowing my clothes?" cried Mamma Cat.

"And who's been in my chest of drawers, borrowing my clothes?" yelled Father Cat.

"And someone's been in my sewing basket too," said Mamma Cat.

"And my coveralls are missing," said Father Cat.

They soon found five very guilty-looking spies.

"It's lucky you spies are in disguise," said Father Cat, trying not to smile. "If I knew which of you was which, I'd have to give you a serious talking-to."

The little kittens scampered off to put their disguises away. I'll bet *you* could tell which was which, couldn't you? But don't tell Father Cat!

35

Huggie's Hat

All the little kittens loved to visit Farmer Feather's farm. There were so many different things to see and do there. And, of course, there was Huggie, too.

Huggie had worked for Farmer Feather for more years than the little kittens could count. He knew everything there was to know about growing crops and looking after animals. The kittens loved to hear his stories about life on the farm years ago, and they liked watching Huggie work as well.

One day, Huggie greeted them with a smile and a wave.

"I've got a job for you little kittens today," he said. "We need a new scarecrow in the top field. I thought you might want to make him for me. Here are some sticks to make him stand up straight. You can fill these sacks with straw to make his head and body, and here are some old clothes to dress him in when you're finished. Have fun!"

The kittens loved making the scarecrow. Honeybun had some crayons in his pocket, so they drew a happy face on the scarecrow's head. They made sure that they put lots of straw in his tummy so he looked fat and jolly.

It wasn't easy dressing the scarecrow. He

seemed as wriggly as a baby kitten. When they were finished, the kittens looked at their creation.

"Something about him isn't right," said Tiger Tail.

"His legs are too thin," said Mopsy. "Let's stuff them with straw. We can tie the bottoms with string."

When the scarecrow's legs were fatter, he looked just right. Huggie came in to have a look.

"That's wonderful," he said, scratching his head. "He looks a little like me! Now you can take him into the middle of the field and push him into the ground."

But Fluffy was still frowning after Huggie had left.

"There's something missing," she said. "He needs a hat!"

"There wasn't a hat with the clothes," said Tiger Tail.

Then all the kittens noticed that Huggie had left his battered old hat behind. It was perfect!

Later that afternoon, the scarecrow watched as the kittens started out for home.

"See you again soon," called Huggie. "You haven't seen my hat anywhere, have you?"

A Fishy Tale

One late summer day, Honeybun decided to go down to the river to see if anything exciting was happening there. But when he mentioned it at breakfast, Mamma Cat put her paw down.

"Water is dangerous," she said, "even for young kittens who are good swimmers. You must never go down to the river without a grown-up cat. And that goes for you others, too."

Honeybun was really disappointed. It was just the kind of sunny, breezy, soft day when it is fun to be near the water.

Just then, he saw Farmer Feather going past in the lane. He was dressed rather strangely and carrying a long pole. Honeybun forgot about the river and ran out to see where his friend was going.

"I'm off to the river to do some fishing," said Farmer Feather. "Would you like to come, too?"

Honeybun couldn't believe his furry little ears. He ran inside to tell Mamma right away.

"As long as you stay with Farmer Feather, that's fine," she said. "Bring us back a fish for our supper!"

Honeybun skipped along the road beside Farmer Feather, but the older cat shook his head.

"I don't want any skipping and jumping when we're near the river, young kitten. You'll frighten the fish away!"

They soon reached the riverbank. Farmer Feather set up his fishing rod and a large green umbrella. Then he reeled out his line and sat down.

Honeybun sat down, too. "What happens now?" he asked.

"We wait," said the farmer. "Ssssh!"

Honeybun waited for *ages*.

"Now what do we do?"

"We wait some more. Sssh!"

Honeybun waited as long as he could.

"If you don't stop wriggling, you'll have to go home," said Farmer Feather.

"How much longer do we have to wait?" asked Honeybun.

"Who knows? An hour or two? Or three? Or four?"

Honeybun sat still for a moment. "I've just remembered something very important I've got to do," he said.

"What, no fish?" called Mamma Cat, later at home.

"It was hopeless," said Honeybun. "Farmer Feather kept *talking*, and he scared them all away!"

The Squiggly Thing

One morning, Rolypoly pushed his bowl away at breakfast. That wasn't like him at all!

"What's the matter, Rolypoly?" asked Mamma Cat.

"I don't want it," said Rolypoly.

"Why not?" Mamma Cat felt her son's furry forehead. "Do you feel sick?"

"Noooo," said Rolypoly slowly. "I'm all right."

"What is it, then?" asked Mamma.

"Can I whisper?" asked the little kitten.

So Rolypoly climbed onto Mamma Cat's lap and whispered in her ear. He didn't want the other little kittens to hear.

"I've got a squiggly thing in my tummy!" he said.

"A squiggly thing?" said Mamma. "What have you been eating, Rolypoly?" She carried the kitten over to the window where they could talk quietly.

"Nothing," whispered her son. "It's just a very wriggly, squiggly thing."

Mamma Cat looked at him carefully.

"Is it wriggling and squiggling all the time?" she asked.

"No," said Rolypoly, "only when I think about my reading test."

Then Mamma Cat understood. Some of the little kittens had a reading test at school that morning, and it was making Rolypoly nervous. The squiggly thing was just nervousness in his tummy.

"But Rolypoly," said Mamma, "you read beautifully. You haven't been worried before, have you?"

"No, but Tiger Tail told me that this was a Really Important Test and he has been feeling terribly worried about it."

Mamma Cat looked across at Tiger Tail.

"He doesn't look very worried to me," she said. "He's got marmalade all over his whiskers and butter on his paws. I think Tiger Tail has been very naughty to make you so worried. I will talk to him later. Now, Rolypoly, you just do your best on the test. That's all you can possibly do. And I will be proud of you no matter how you do."

Then Mamma Cat gave Rolypoly a big hug, and the little kitten found that the squiggly thing had wriggled right away.

That afternoon, the little kittens were all cheering Rolypoly when they came home from school.

"He got the highest mark," said Mopsy. "Isn't that good?"

"That's wonderful!" said Mamma Cat. "And how did Tiger Tail do?"

"Not very well," said Mopsy. "I think he's hiding."

"I'll find him," said Mamma Cat. "I need to have words with that young kitten." Can you find him first?

Alfred to the Rescue

One morning, the little kittens were playing outside, while Mamma Cat sat in the sunshine and shelled some peas. Father Cat had borrowed Farmer Feather's new ladder (he had lost his old one around the time the kittens built their treehouse) to paint the upstairs windows.

Just then, a little kitten went past in the lane and waved to Mamma Cat's family. The kittens ignored him.

"Who was that?" asked Mamma Cat.

"Oh," said Fluffy, "that was Alfred. He's new at school."

"Why didn't you ask him to come and play?" asked Mamma. "He looked like a nice little kitten to me."

"Oh, he wouldn't want to play with us," said Tiger Tail. "The teacher is always saying how smart he is."

"Well, all my kittens are smart in their own ways," said Mamma Cat. "I hope you're not being unkind. I thought Alfred looked a little lonely."

Half an hour later, the kittens were playing an exciting game of chase-the-tail.

"Careful!" warned Father Cat, high up on his ladder. "You almost made me wobble!"

But Tiger Tail, tearing around the corner of the house, didn't hear him.

Crash! He knocked the ladder sideways. Father Cat lost his footing. As he grabbed the top of the window, his paint can sailed up into the air and down again, landing on his head.

"Help!" cried Father Cat. "I can't see a thing!"

"Help!" cried Mamma Cat. "What can we do?"

"Help!" cried the little kittens. "He's going to fall."

"Keep calm!" cried a voice from the lane. It was Alfred, and he took charge at once.

"I'm going to talk you down, Mr. Cat," he said. "Just do exactly what I say. Now move your right paw a little to the left...."

In next to no time, Alfred had saved the day. Everyone was so happy that Father Cat was safe that they didn't scold the little kittens. But everyone wanted to congratulate Alfred and be his friend.

"I'm just glad you weren't hurt, Mr. Cat," said Alfred.

"Not hurt," giggled Mamma Cat, "but a lovely shade of lavender. It's very becoming, dear!"

Aunt Amelia

amma Cat was surprised when Mrs. Mumbles stopped her in the street one Saturday morning. Mrs. Mumbles was the little kittens' schoolteacher.

"I was just wondering, Mrs. Cat," said Mrs. Mumbles in sympathetic tones, "how your dear sister is now. The kittens have been so worried about her. I do understand that they find it hard to concentrate in class when she is on their minds."

"My sister?" said Mamma faintly.

"Yes," said Mrs. Mumbles, "the kittens' Aunt Amelia. I do hope there is good news."

"Excellent news," said Mamma Cat briskly. "She has made a remarkable recovery and went home this morning. I'm glad to say that the kittens don't need to worry anymore. In fact, I'm sure they will want to work extra hard next week to catch up on their work."

"I can help them with that," said Mrs. Mumbles. "Do tell your sister how glad I am that she's better. Good-bye!"

"Good-bye!" said Mamma Cat. "I will!" And that, you know, was very strange, because although Mamma Cat has six brothers, she has no sisters at all.

But while Mamma Cat was walking home, she decided that maybe she *did* have a sister after all. She walked home and beamed at her kittens, who were trying to do acrobatics on the grass.

"My dears," said Mamma, "I have wonderful news! Your Aunt Amelia, who has been so ill, is much better now and is coming to stay with us!"

The kittens looked at each other. They knew perfectly well that Tiger Tail and Honeybun had invented Aunt Amelia on the spur of the moment when they were faced with an extra-long spelling test. Since then, she had become very useful indeed. But what did Mamma mean? How could a make-believe aunt come to stay?"

"Oh, Mamma," said Mopsy. "I don't understand. How *can* Aunt Amelia visit?"

"Well, why shouldn't she?" asked Mamma

"Well … because … because …" Honeybun didn't quite know how to begin.

"Because there isn't a real Aunt Amelia," said Tiger Tail. "We made her up, Mamma. I'm sorry."

"I know," said Mamma. "And if you naughty little kittens aren't *very* good over the next few weeks, Mrs. Mumbles will know too."

"We'll be good!" chorused the little kittens. After all, Mrs. Mumbles is a very intelligent cat, who knows a very great deal, but she doesn't need to know *everything*!

Katie's Clock

Mamma Cat did her best to make sure that her little kittens were never late for school. She kept a sharp eye on the clock in the mornings.

Unfortunately, Katie Kitten, who lived next door, was nearly always late. Her mother had not five but twelve little kittens to look after. It was not surprising that she often forgot to wind the clock, so it nearly always showed the wrong time.

After a while, Mrs. Mumbles lost patience with poor Katie.

"Katie Kitten!" she said. "You are late again. Don't you have a watch?"

"No, Mrs. Mumbles," said Katie.

"Oh," said Mrs. Mumbles, "well, please try to be more punctual in the future."

Next morning, Katie was not just on time—she was early!

"I've got something better than a watch," she smiled, "but it's a secret."

For the rest of that week, Katie was on time. Mrs. Mumbles was very pleased.

The following Monday, Katie was at school bright and early again. That morning, Mrs. Mumbles gave the class a multiplication test.

"I want absolute silence," she said.

But it seemed that absolute silence was difficult to find. First one of Farmer Feather's noisiest tractors rumbled slowly by in the lane. Then a dog trotted by, barking loudly.

"Don't be distracted, class," said Mrs. Mumbles. "Hopefully, we'll have peace now."

But just then … *drriiiiiiing! drriiiiiiing! drriiiiiiing!* Mrs. Mumbles nearly jumped out of her fur. She looked around the class. One little kitten was looking very pink. It was Katie.

"I'm sorry," she said. "I've been bringing my Granny's alarm clock, so that I'm not late."

"Katie," said Mrs. Mumbles, "You are not to bring an alarm clock to school again."

That evening, the kittens told Mamma Cat what had happened. Later, when they were in bed, Mamma Cat left Father Cat in charge and slipped out on an errand, carrying a box from her jewelry drawer.

Much to the kittens' surprise, Katie was on time again the next morning.

"Look!" she said. "A surprise present came through the door last night. It's a watch! I wish I knew where it came from."

I think that's our secret, don't you?

Splish! Splash!

Mamma Cat sighed as she looked at the dirty dishes by the sink. "Oh dear," she groaned, "I do *hate* washing dishes!"

"We'll do it for you, Mamma," said Mopsy, ignoring nudges from Tiger Tail on one side and Rolypoly on the other.

"Are you sure you can manage?" asked Mamma, looking surprised and a little anxious.

Mopsy tried to look grown up and sensible. "Of course we can," she said.

Mamma Cat was very tired, so she stopped listening to the little warning voice in her head. She went into the living room and put her paws up. Soon she was fast asleep.

Reluctantly, Fluffy and Rolypoly cleared the rest of the dishes from the kitchen table. Tiger Tail took charge of the sink … and turned on the water so hard that everyone was soaked. Meanwhile, Mopsy squeezed just a little too much dishwashing liquid into the sink.

"What lovely bubbles!" squealed Fluffy. "We could have a bubble-blowing contest!"

For ten minutes, the dishwashing was forgotten as five little kittens chased bubbles around the kitchen. By the time they'd finished, they had to squeeze more bubbles into the sink because the others were used up.

At last Honeybun began washing the dishes. Fluffy and Mopsy dried, and Rolypoly and Tiger Tail put the cups, plates, knives, forks, and spoons away.

The floor was fairly slippery by now, with all the spilled water and bubbles, so it wasn't really Rolypoly's fault when he fell over and a few things got broken.

When everything was put away, Tiger Tail said, "There's still lots of bubbly water. What do you think we should do with it?" It did seem a shame to waste it, so he and Mopsy ran upstairs to find their bath toys.

When Mamma Cat came in a few minutes later, she suddenly felt much more tired than she had before.

"We can't understand why you don't like washing dishes, Mamma," cried the five little kittens. "We think it's lots of fun!"

The Pumpkin Prize

For weeks, Father Cat had a determined look on his face. "This year," he said, "I'm going to do it. Oh yes."

"Does it really matter?" asked Mamma Cat. "It's only a little prize."

"It's not the prize. It's the principle," said Father Cat sternly, reaching for his watering can.

It was the time of year when the local Fruit and Vegetable Show was only weeks away. For more years than he cared to remember, Father Cat had tried to win the Pumpkin Prize. It was for the biggest, roundest, brightest orange pumpkin in the show. And for just as many years, the biggest, roundest, brightest orange pumpkin had been grown by Farmer Feather. Father Cat and Farmer Feather were the best of friends, but at this time of year, they only muttered to each other as they passed. They were deadly rivals.

This year, the kittens had bought Father Cat a special book for his birthday. It was called *Expert Pumpkin Growing*. There was only one problem. Father Cat wasn't an expert. He couldn't understand the book, which was full of the longest words he had ever seen.

Maybe just owning the book was enough, for that year Father Cat managed to grow a really huge orange pumpkin.

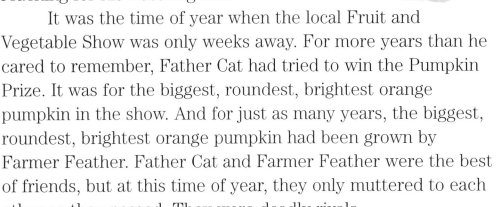

Long before the show, he realized that his wheelbarrow would not be big enough to carry it, so he made a special little cart.

On the morning of the show, the little kittens and Mamma Cat all gathered to help Father Cat load the pumpkin.

"Left a bit. Right a bit. Careful!" called Father Cat, as the pumpkin was rolled onto the cart. It was much too heavy to lift.

"I'll open the gate," said Honeybun, running down the path.

But opening the gate did not help. The pumpkin was much wider than the cart or the gate. It just would not go through.

"Oh dear, what a shame," said Father Cat. "It would probably have won the prize, but it will have to stay in the garden. Never mind."

Mamma Cat and the little kittens couldn't believe that Father Cat was taking it all so well. But then, they hadn't seen what he had just seen, far away in one of Farmer Feather's fields, had they?

The Christmas Kittens

It was the coldest, snowiest Christmas Mamma and Father Cat could remember. The little kittens loved it. They made snowcats and had snowball fights. Then, when the light began to fade in the afternoon and even their whiskers felt a little frosty, they would hurry inside for hot chocolate and one of Mamma Cat's special little mince pies.

"This is perfect weather for Christmas," sighed Fluffy, gazing out of the window at the best snowcat she had made yet. "And there are only three days to go!" She couldn't keep a little squeak of excitement out of her voice.

"I'd rather be staying with my cousin Fred in Australia," muttered Father Cat, who had had enough of clearing snow from the path and getting icicles in his ears. "He'll be sitting on the beach in the sunshine on Christmas Day, *and* he'll have warm ears!"

"You know," said Mamma Cat, "we are very lucky to have such a nice, warm home at Christmastime, even if it is cold outside. Some cats and kittens are not so lucky. I think we should ask another family to join us on Christmas Day, to share our dinner."

"No!" said Father Cat. "Five little kittens squealing over their presents and getting tired and tearful are enough!"

"No!" said Mopsy. "Strange kittens might break my new toys."

"No!" said Rolypoly. "Other kittens would eat *my* little mince pie."

"No!" said Tiger Tail. "If we have visitors, we'll have to be *quiet*."

"No!" said Honeybun. "It's fun with just us here."

"Well," said Fluffy, "I'm not sure it would be fun if we were thinking about poor little kittens who aren't so lucky all the time."

"We wouldn't be," said Mopsy.

"I would," sighed Fluffy.

"So would I," said Mamma Cat.

"Well, if you put it like that…" muttered Father Cat.

"I suppose there *are* enough mince pies," said Rolypoly.

So that was why there were *eleven* little kittens around the Christmas table that year. And those kittens *did* get tired and tearful. And Mopsy's new bicycle *did* get broken (and fixed again by Father Cat). And *all* the mince pies were eaten. And Tiger Tail was not at all quiet. And everyone had the best Christmas *ever*!

A New Friend

The little kittens were not very happy when they heard that Great Aunt Florence was coming to stay.

"Remember," said Mamma Cat, "Great Aunt Florence is not a young cat. She will need peace and quiet more than anything else. There must be no shouting, Rolypoly. No running around, Tiger Tail. No squealing, Fluffy. No talking with your mouth full, Rolypoly. And no yelling, Mopsy. Do you understand?"

"Yes, Mamma," said the little kittens, but they could feel their whiskers drooping. They imagined a very old, frail cat sitting in a chair with a shawl around her shoulders and a blanket around her knees. There would be no fun in the house at all while she was staying.

But when Great Aunt Florence arrived, she wasn't at all like they had expected.

"Great Aunt Florence is such a mouthful," she said. "Call me Flo!"

Flo wore lots and lots of beads and bangles. (And they sometimes dangled in her soup!)

Flo wore extraordinary clothes with frills and flounces. (And they sometimes got caught on the door handles!)

Flo spoke in a loud voice and used words that made Father Cat shudder and the little kittens giggle!

Still, the little kittens remembered what Mamma had said, and they tried hard to be good and quiet. They did their very best for three days, before Tiger Tail said, "I can't stand this anymore. Let's go right to the end of the orchard, where no one can hear us, and have a good game of soccer. I might burst if I can't shout and run around."

The other little kittens didn't need persuading. In less than a minute they were under the apple trees, having a really exciting game.

When Great Aunt Florence appeared suddenly from behind a flower bed, the kittens felt a little ashamed. They had been being very noisy. But Flo had a sparkle in her eye.

"Well, well, soccer!" she cried. "I was beginning to worry about you kittens. You were so good and quiet."

She took off her big hat and tossed it into a tree.

Flo expertly kicked the ball right at her hat. "GOAL!" she yelled. "Catch me if you can!"

A Terrible Tangle

Mamma Cat was knitting squares as if her life depended on it. They were very small squares, and the little kittens were all very puzzled by them.

"Maybe they're blankets for baby rabbits," said Mopsy, who had been reading a story about bunnies.

"They could be dishcloths," said Rolypoly, looking bored.

"No one," said Fluffy, "could need so many dishcloths. I think they're little shawls for dolls."

Mamma Cat looked up and smiled. "The squares are going to be joined together," she said, "to make a big bright blanket. I'm making one, and Mrs. Willow is making one. I'm determined to finish first."

The little kittens didn't like Mrs. Willow much.

"Let us help you, Mamma!" said Fluffy. "You're sure to win then."

Mamma looked a little doubtful, but the kittens looked so eager, she agreed at last.

"I'm using yarn from some old sweaters you've outgrown," she said. "All you have to do is unravel them by pulling gently, like this, and wind the yarn into little balls."

"We can do that!" cried the kittens. It looked like fun.

"I'll just go and put dinner in the oven," said Mamma Cat. "Just call me if you need help."

But the little kittens were enjoying themselves too much to call when things began to go ever so slightly wrong. When Mamma Cat walked back into the room, she couldn't believe the sight that met her eyes. Bright yarn was crisscrossing the room in all directions. It was hanging from the lamp and twirling around the furniture.

"Oh no!" groaned Mamma Cat.

But when Tiger Tail saw how upset Mamma was, he had a good idea.

"There will be a special prize," he announced, "for the kitten who winds up all of his or her ball first."

Who do you think won? And who is in danger of undoing all of Mamma's hard work?

What's My Name?

One evening, Mamma Cat read the little kittens a story they had never heard before. It was about a funny little man who helped a girl marry the King. In return, he asked for her first baby. Of course, when the time came, the Queen did not want to give up her baby. The little man told her that he would disappear forever if she could guess his name. You probably know this story already. It is called "Rumpelstiltskin".

The next day, the little kittens were still thinking about the story.

"It was lucky the Queen managed to find out the name," said Mopsy. "She would never have been able to guess it."

"Nonsense!" cried Tiger Tail. "I bet I could have guessed it. You could see from the pictures that the little man looked just like someone who would be called Rumpelstiltskin."

"Is that so?" asked Mamma Cat. "So you wouldn't have any trouble guessing your *father's* name then?"

"But we know his name," said Fluffy. "It's Charles."

"Yes," said Mamma Cat. "But his full name is Charles F. Cat. Do you know what the *F* stands for?"

"Now, now, we don't need to go into that," muttered Father Cat from behind his newspaper.

But the little kittens were curious now.

"Is it Ferdinand, Frederick, Francis, or Felix?" they asked.

"No," said Father Cat.

"Is it Finton, Felipe, Forrest, or Fingle?" asked the kittens.

"No," said Father Cat.

"Is it Floozle, Fenugreek, Fandangle, or Finklefog?" asked Tiger Tail.

"*No!*" cried Father Cat.

For days, the kittens tried to guess. They spent more time with their encyclopedias and dictionaries than Mrs. Mumbles their teacher had ever been able to persuade them to do before. At last, after the fifth dinnertime at which Father Cat had been bombarded with very unlikely-sounding names beginning with *F*, he put his paw down.

"There will be no more guessing about my name," he said. "It's a very silly name. My parents were just not concentrating at the time. I have no intention of telling you … ever!"

"Now, dear," said Mamma Cat. "I think it's a sweet name. After all, you did use it for one of your own children."

At that, the kittens burst out laughing and Father Cat rushed out to his vegetable garden with pink ears! Can you guess Father Cat's full name now?

Open House

Mamma Cat sighed and looked at her appointment book. "I don't know what we're going to do," she said. "We've been invited out by lots of cats recently, and we must ask them to visit us in return. But I just can't see how we're going to fit them all in."

Just then, Tiger Tail came tearing through the house like a whirlwind.

"I can't stop!" he called. "I've got to go and finish my project for the school Open Day."

That gave Mamma Cat an idea.

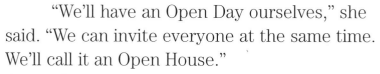

"We'll have an Open Day ourselves," she said. "We can invite everyone at the same time. We'll call it an Open House."

"Good idea," mumbled Father Cat, who was munching a sandwich. "You arrange it, dear. Invite whoever you like."

"I certainly will," said Mamma Cat, "but you are going to have to fix the hinges on the front door. It feels very wobbly every time I open it. We can't have it coming off in a visitor's paw."

"I'll do it tonight," said Father Cat. But, you know, with one thing and another, Father Cat never did get around to fixing the door....

The day of the Open House was warm and sunny. Mamma Cat prepared enormous amounts of delicious food. The little cats helped put it on the table, only eating a tiny bit on the way. Fluffy and Rolypoly gathered flowers to decorate the living room and arranged them in every free vase, bottle, and mug they could find. Honeybun and Mopsy folded paper napkins into the most amazing shapes. As for Tiger Tail, he was rushing here and there, and no one was very sure *what* he was doing.

It was only when the guests began to arrive that a guilty look came over Father Cat's face. He remembered that he had not fixed the door. As each visitor came in, he held his breath, but the door, though wobbly, stayed firmly in place. When the last cat had arrived, Father Cat gave a sigh of relief.

But just then, Tiger Tail came tearing in from outside. The door gave a wobble and a wibble and made an *eeeeeeeeeah* sound. Then it fell right off its hinges and out onto the path.

There was a deafening silence. Then Father Cat gave a little laugh.

"Well, it really is an Open House now!" he chuckled.

The Honey Pot

 One afternoon, Farmer Feather brought Mamma Cat a huge pot of honey. It was a pretty blue pot, filled to the brim with lovely golden honey from Farmer Feather's own bees.

"It's funny," he said. "My wife and I have had so much honey recently, we just don't seem to enjoy it anymore. I hope your hungry little ones will like this."

"I'm sure they will," said Mamma Cat. "Thank you very much, Farmer Feather."

When Tiger Tail saw the honey pot, he wanted to dip his little paw in right away.

"Just one little taste, Mamma!" he pleaded, but Mamma Cat was firm.

"I don't want sticky pawmarks all over the house," she said. "You can have some tomorrow, like everyone else."

That evening, Mamma Cat had no peace. Each little kitten in turn begged to be able to dip just one little paw into the honey. Even Father Cat was discovered lifting up the lid.

"No," said Mamma. "You will all have to wait until tomorrow."

Of course, that just made the rest of the family long to taste that honey even more. As she turned out the lights before bed that night, Mamma Cat herself couldn't resist taking a peek inside. And when she saw the golden honey, she dipped her paw just a little way into it. Mmmmm!

That night, one little kitten after another discovered that it was very hard to sleep without a taste of that honey. One by one, they crept into the kitchen and had just one—or maybe two—or maybe several more—tastes of the yummy sweet, sticky stuff. Even Father Cat slipped out of bed when the moon was high in the sky, and I'm sorry to say that he had *quite a few* tastes.

Next day, Mamma Cat saw sticky pawmarks on the kitchen door. She was pretty sure she knew what had happened, but she didn't feel she could scold anyone, as she had tasted the honey herself.

That evening at supper, Mamma announced, "Now you can all have as much honey as you like on your bread and butter."

"No thank you," said the little kittens. "We don't really feel like it today."

"What about you, dear?" asked Mamma Cat, turning to her husband.

"Not tonight, perhaps," he said.

Then Mamma lifted the lid of the honey pot with a smile.

"It's a good thing we all had a taste yesterday," she said, "because there isn't any left at *all* today!"

Three Little Kittens

For several days, Mamma Cat and Father Cat had been whispering together and exchanging smiles. The little kittens wondered if they were planning a surprise party or thinking of taking the whole family on an exciting trip.

But day after day, nothing happened, and the kittens began to feel as if they were being left out of a secret. Maybe that is why they were all being noisier and more trouble than usual.

One evening, as Mamma sat in her chair with her feet up, Tiger Tail rushed through and upset her cup of coffee all over the floor. Honeybun, who was not paying attention, ran into the room and skidded right into the puddle of coffee. He fell down with a bump and knocked over a vase of flowers. Fluffy, reading a book, walked through the mess and left wet pawprints all the way into the kitchen. Rolypoly tripped over Honeybun, and Mopsy, coming to see what all the noise was about, fell over *him* and landed in Mamma's lap.

"Oh my goodness," cried Mamma, "this is too much! You kittens are going to have to learn to be quieter and more gentle. I can't put up with this!"

The little kittens were not used to seeing Mamma so upset. They hurried to clean up the mess and bring her a new cup of coffee. Meanwhile, Mamma had been thinking.

"My cousin Mildred has just had some new kittens," she said. "I'll ask her to stay. Then you will have to be quiet and careful."

Cousin Mildred's new kittens were tiny! Tiger Tail was the only little kitten at home when she arrived. At first, he was afraid to go near them, but Mamma Cat and Mildred only had one pair of paws each, so when all three baby kittens were crying, he decided to help. And strangely enough, he found that it was really nice to cuddle a little furry bundle.

When Fluffy and Honeybun came running in a few minutes later, Tiger Tail looked fierce.

"Shhh!" he said. "You mustn't disturb the babies. Please try to be more thoughtful. And please wait outside for Rolypoly and Mopsy, so that they don't come bursting in and making noise."

Later, as the little kittens took turns cuddling the babies, Tiger Tail had a good idea.

"Can't we have some little brothers and sisters, Mamma?" he asked.

Mamma Cat and Father Cat exchanged a smile.

"We'll see," said Mamma.

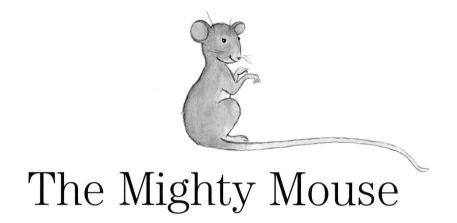

The Mighty Mouse

One morning at school, Mrs. Mumbles told the little kittens all about mice. Now kittens and cats are very interested in mice, as you can imagine, but these days, with good home cooking and lots of stores where cats can buy food, many younger kittens have never come face to face with a real live mouse.

In the playground after the lesson, Bella was pretending to know everything as usual.

"Ordinary mice are no problem," she said. "What you need to worry about are *giant* mice. They are twice as big as a grown-up cat and twice as fierce. If you meet one of those mighty mice, there is no escape!"

The little kittens were impressed by this. They tried to imagine what a giant mouse might look like, but since they had never seen even an ordinary mouse, they found it somewhat difficult.

"They have long tails and whiskers," said Mopsy. "I read it in my book."

"I hope I never meet one—a giant one, I mean," said Fluffy with a shudder.

"Ugh! Let's not talk about it," said Honeybun. "The whole idea gives me the shivers."

So the little kittens did not talk about giant mice anymore, but all of them were thinking about just how big those giant tails and whiskers might be.

That evening, Rolypoly tossed and turned in his bed. Every time he closed his eyes, he seemed to see the staring eyes of a monster that just might be a giant mouse. At last, unable to sleep, he crept out of bed and tiptoed toward the kitchen. There was a little lamp shining in the hallway.

As Rolypoly padded along quietly, he happened to glance over his shoulder.

"Aaaaaah!" he squeaked, his little heart thudding. There on the wall was a giant shadow. It had whiskers! It had a tail! It was a giant mouse, and it was right behind him!

With another squeal, Rolypoly ran into the living room. There was Mamma eating a strange snack of banana and sardine sandwiches, as she often did these days.

"What on earth is the matter?" she gasped.

Rolypoly buried his face in Mamma's skirt, expecting at any minute to hear the thud of giant feet behind him. But when he told Mamma what had happened, she laughed.

"Come with me, Rolypoly," she said, leading him into the hallway, where there were now *two* giant shadows on the wall. "Wiggle your whiskers!" said Mamma. And what do you think Rolypoly saw?

Five More Minutes

Mamma Cat put down her knitting. "Time for bed, kittens," she said. "Fluffy, don't forget to brush your teeth. Honeybun, remember to wash behind your ears."

But before Mamma could finish what she was saying, all the little kittens cried out together, "Oh no, Mamma, just five more minutes, please!"

Mamma looked at her kittens. Two of them were painting pictures, one was reading a book, and the other two were playing a quiet game of tiddlywinks.

"All right," she said. "Just five more minutes. Then it is *definitely* bedtime."

She looked up at the clock as she spoke and noticed that it said seven-thirty. Mamma sighed and sipped her cocoa, glad to have another few minutes' peace before all the dashing and splashing that always happened before her kittens were settled down for the night.

Maybe it was the cocoa, or maybe it was just because Mamma was so tired these days, but before long the little kittens noticed that Mamma Cat had fallen asleep.

"Ssssh!" said Mopsy. "If we keep quiet, she may sleep for a long time, and we can stay up late!"

Mamma did sleep for about fifteen minutes. Then she began to stretch and yawn. Quick as a flash, and as quietly as his paws would carry him, Tiger Tail crept over to the clock. He turned the hands back to seven-thirty!

When Mamma Cat woke up, she turned to her kittens at once.

"Time for bed," she said firmly. "Then I can get some rest, too."

"But Mamma," said Tiger Tail, "you said we could have five more minutes!"

Mamma looked at the clock. She knew she'd been asleep, but it looked as if no time had passed at all. Just a minute! Wasn't that a painty pawmark on the clock?

Mamma smiled. "I've poured you some glasses of milk in the kitchen," she said. "Run along and drink them."

The kittens ran out of the room. Quick as a flash, and just as quietly as Tiger Tail, Mamma ran over to the clock and moved the hands forward.

As five pairs of milky whiskers returned, she called out, "Bedtime *now*, kittens! It's half past midnight!"

The little kittens knew that Mamma had played a trick on them, but they couldn't say anything without admitting they had tried it, too.

"Good night, Mamma," they said.

"Sleep tight, kittens," smiled Mamma.

The Biggest Balloon

The five little kittens were very excited. They were getting ready for their birthday party.

"Quiet, please!" called Mamma, who was busy trying to decorate five special birthday cakes to please her five kittens. "Honeybun, be careful with those streamers! Mopsy, it's much too early to be wearing your party dress. Tiger Tail, what are you doing with those balloons?"

"I'm going to blow them all up, Mamma," said Tiger Tail. "I thought it would be helpful."

"It would, sweetheart," said Mamma, "but you'll run out of breath if you try to do them all yourself. Why don't you all take a break from what you're doing and blow up balloons together?"

Of course, as soon as all the little kittens began blowing up balloons, they each tried to outdo the others.

"My balloons are the biggest!" called Tiger Tail. "This one is huge!"

Rolypoly looked at his brother's balloon. He was pretty sure he could blow up a bigger one. Between puffs, he pinched the neck of the balloon tightly between his paws, so the air wouldn't escape.

"This one is big … *puff!*" he gasped, and took a deep breath. "It's bigger than Mopsy's … *puff!* … It's bigger than Fluffy's … *puff!* … It's bigger than Honeybun's … *puff!* … It's even … bigger … than … *puff!* … Tiger Tail's! Just … one … more … puff … and …" Before Rolypoly could finish his sentence, there was a loud *POP!*

Rolypoly's burst balloon shot across the room and fell … *plop!* … right on top of one of the birthday cakes.

"Luckily, that was your cake, Rolypoly," said Mamma, picking the floppy balloon off the frosting. "Did you make a wish?"

Kittens always make a wish when a balloon goes pop.

"I wished for roller skates," said Rolypoly.

"I wished for a nurse's costume," said Fluffy.

"I wished for a book about caterpillars," said Mopsy.

"I wished for a building set," said Honeybun.

"I wished for a baby brother," said Tiger Tail. He had not forgotten the time his tiny cousins came to stay.

Mamma Cat laughed, thinking about the presents already wrapped up and hidden carefully under her bed.

"Well, maybe your wishes will come true," she said.

"Even mine?" whispered Tiger Tail, coming to taste a sticky spoon.

"That would be telling," smiled Mamma Cat.

The Cat in the Moon

One spring evening, Father Cat took all the little kittens outside to look at the stars. He told them that the stars were millions and millions of miles away.

"And look," said Mopsy. "There's the famous cat in the moon!"

All the kittens looked. Sure enough, there *was* the shape of a cat on the face of the silvery moon.

But Tiger Tail hung his head.

"I can't see it," he said.

Patiently, Father Cat tried to show Tiger Tail where the cat was, but Tiger Tail made an excuse and went inside.

Father Cat had a word with Mamma, and they kept an eye on Tiger Tail over the next few days.

At last, Mamma Cat took her little kitten on one side.

"I'm going to take you to have your eyes tested," she said. "It won't hurt a bit, and it might explain why you've broken so many plates and cups and windows recently."

Tiger Tail didn't really want to go, but the idea of an afternoon away from school appealed to him.

Mr. Specks the eye doctor looked carefully at Tiger Tail's eyes and asked him to read some letters on a chart.

"Well, young kitten," he said, "you need a pair of glasses."

Tiger Tail was horrified. He silently promised himself that he wouldn't wear them, *ever*. He didn't say a word to the other little kittens.

The following week, Mamma and Tiger Tail went to pick up the glasses.

Tiger Tail wrinkled up his nose and refused to open his eyes as Mr. Specks fitted them. Then he took just a little peek, and cried out.

"I can see a bee on the window! I can see a penny on the floor! Oh, and when I look in the mirror, I can see *me*!"

Tiger Tail was so pleased with his bright new world that he didn't give another thought to the glasses on his nose, even when the other little kittens looked at him curiously.

That night, the little kittens went out to look at the stars again.

"Can you see the cat in the moon now, Tiger?" asked Father Cat.

"Oh yes," said the little kitten, with a mischievous look at his brothers and sisters. "These glasses are so good that I can see him waving to me!"

Well, those other little kittens have been pestering Mamma Cat for glasses of their own for weeks now. As for Tiger Tail, he is much happier, although I'm sorry to say that cups and plates and windows are still not safe from that lively little kitten.

The Quacking Kitten

Farmer Feather met Father Cat in the lane. The two pumpkin-growing rivals were good friends again now.

"How are things with you and your family?" asked Farmer Feather.

"As chaotic as usual," smiled Father Cat. "How are things on the farm?"

"Oh, I love this time of year," smiled Farmer Feather. "There is always so much going on in the spring, with new little ones popping up all over the place."

"Yes, indeed," said Father Cat.

"Perhaps your little kittens would like to come down to the barnyard," said the kind farmer. "There are lots of little chicks and ducklings hatching out just now. But you will warn them to be quiet, won't you?"

"Well, I'll try," said Father Cat very doubtfully.

The little kittens were delighted to be visiting the farm.

"I love baby animals," said Tiger Tail wistfully.

"You will remember to be quiet and gentle, won't you?" called Father Cat, but the little kittens were already running down the path.

As soon as they reached the barnyard, the kittens could see that it was fully of hurrying and scurrying and a sense of excitement.

"Oh, look!" cried Mopsy, running forward. A mother hen was proudly leading her six fluffy little chicks across the yard.

But Tiger Tail had seen something even more exciting. Down by the pond, a mother duck was standing over her nest. In front of her were three eggs—and there were cracks in them! Tiger Tail watched in wonder as first one, then two, then three little heads popped out of the eggs.

As they shook their feathers in the sunshine, the three little ducklings looked around. And the first thing they saw was Tiger Tail.

The little kitten smiled. "Quack!" he said in a friendly way. "Quack! Quack!"

With a squawk of excitement, the ducklings waddled off their nest and looked up at Tiger Tail. They thought he was their mother! When Tiger Tail walked away from the pond, the ducklings followed. When he walked toward the gate, they followed again.

"I see my hens and ducks are not the only ones to have new families," laughed Farmer Feather. "How much do you know about raising ducklings, young kitten? There's no need to look so worried. I'll just scoop these little ones up and you can escape. If you had been quiet, this wouldn't have happened."

Tiger Tail *was* fairly quiet on the way home.

"It would have been nice to have some ducklings," he said.

"Tiger Tail," laughed Fluffy, "you're … *quackers*!"

First Day of School

Mrs. Mumbles was in a brisk mood as she hurried her kittens into school one Monday morning.

"Come along now," she said. "I want you all to go straight to your places and show how well you can behave. We have two new kittens joining us this morning. They have just moved into the house at the end of Blueberry Lane."

The teacher urged two kittens in blue dresses toward the front of the class.

"Here are Daisy and Maisy," she said. "Or is it Maisy and Daisy?"

The new kittens were twins! Fluffy looked as closely as she could without being rude, but she simply could not tell them apart.

As the morning wore on, it became obvious that no one else could either, including Mrs. Mumbles. Before long, everyone was completely confused—and the new kittens were grinning from ear to ear.

Honeybun, who had been known to get up to a trick or two himself, soon noticed that the twins were having a lot of fun. At lunchtime, the kittens lined up to be given their milk by Mrs. Mumbles.

"Just a minute … er … Maisy," said the teacher, "I've already given you your milk, haven't I?"

"No, Mrs. Mumbles, that was Daisy," said the kitten, looking as sweet as blueberry pie.

But five minutes later, Mrs. Mumbles found herself giving a very similar kitten another glass of milk.

"It *is* easy to get confused, isn't it?" smiled the twin. "I'm afraid you must have given my sister *two* glasses!"

By the end of the day, Mrs. Mumbles' patience was running out, and the other little kittens in the class were giggling as much as Maisy and Daisy.

"I'm sorry, kittens," said the teacher at last. "I don't like to tell pupils what to wear, but you two are just going to have to put on something that will help me tell you apart."

"Oh," said Maisy and Daisy together, "you mean something like this?" And out of the necks of their dresses those two naughty little kittens fished little chains, one with an M and one with a D.

Mrs. Mumbles didn't know whether to be angry or relieved as the whole class broke into laughter. It was a good thing she didn't hear the conversation between Honeybun and Maisy as they put their coats on to go home that afternoon.

"Do you wear those chains all the time?" asked Honeybun.

"Oh yes," said Maisy with a smile, "it's fun deciding which one to wear each morning!"

Kittens to Cuddle

One fine day, Doctor Duckweed came to the little kittens' home. He had a few quiet words with Mamma Cat, rescued his stethoscope from Rolypoly, who was seeing if he could ping balls of paper with it, and waved merrily as he went off down the path.

"Goodbye, Mrs. Cat," he called. "It won't be long now!"

"What's not long now?" asked Tiger Tail.

"Ah," said Mamma, "now, I've been meaning to talk to you about that. Sit down, all of you, and listen."

But just then, Rolypoly sat on the beautiful castle that Honeybun had been building and in the noise and trouble that followed, everyone forgot that Mamma had something important to say.

The next day, Mamma cleaned the house and did a lot of baking. Father Cat helped with the vacuuming.

"Why are we spring cleaning today?" asked Mopsy.

""Well, that's what I was going to talk to you about," Mamma began.

But just then Father Cat vacuumed up Fluffy's crayons, and the vacuum cleaner began to make a strange noise, and Fluffy started to cry, so Mamma never did manage to finish what she was saying.

That night, Mamma Cat told the kittens to go to bed earlier than usual.

"But why, Mamma?" asked Mopsy. "I haven't finished my book."

But just then, Tiger Tail, who was looking into a basket Mamma kept behind her chair, said, "Ooooh!" and "Aaaah!" and "Yes, we'll go to bed now!"

Mamma gave Tiger Tail a secret smile, and Tiger Tail immediately took charge of his brothers and sisters in a very grown-up way. In no time at all, they were all tucked into bed and fast asleep.

All except Tiger Tail, that is. He was much too excited to sleep. In the darkness, he thought he heard some whispering, and a knocking at the door, and even some little tiny meowing noises that made him wriggle his whiskers with happiness before he too closed his eyes.

Tiger Tail was the first little kitten to get up the next morning, but the others were not far behind. Following Tiger Tail, they crept into Mamma's room. She was sitting up in bed with a big smile on her face—and three baby kittens in her arms!

Before long, the five *big* kittens were snuggling on the bed with their baby brothers and sisters.

"They're so sweet," said Father Cat proudly. "We love them to bits."

Tiger Tail whispered in Mamma's furry ear.

"You do still love us too, don't you?"

"More than ever, sweetheart," smiled Mamma. "More than ever."

Index of Themes